D1246481

THE
DRAGONS
CLUB

CYN BERMUDEZ

An imprint of Enslow Publishing

WEST 44 BOOKS™

Please visit our website, www.west44books.com.
For a free color catalog of all our high-quality books,
call toll free 1-800-398-2504.

Cataloging-in-Publication Data
Names: Bermudez, Cyn.
Title: The dragons club / Cyn Bermudez.
Description: New York : West 44, 2023. | Series: West 44 YA
verse
Identifiers: ISBN 9781978596047 (pbk.) | ISBN 9781978596030
(library bound) | ISBN 9781978596054 (ebook)
Subjects: LCSH: American poetry--21st century. | Poetry,
Modern--21st century. | English poetry.
Classification: LCC PS584.B476 2023 | DDC 811'.6--dc23

First Edition

Published in 2023 by
Enslow Publishing LLC
29 East 21st Street
New York, NY 10011

Copyright © 2023 Enslow Publishing LLC

Editor: Caitie McAneney
Designer: Katelyn E. Reynolds

Photo Credits: Cvr, p. 1 Thorsten Schmitt/Shutterstock.com.

Printed in the United States of America

CPSIA compliance information: Batch #CS23W44: For further information contact
Enslow Publishing LLC, New York, New York at 1-800-398-2504.

 VIOLIN

I play my violin:
wind-bow-resin-rain.

An extension of forefinger,
hand, and arm. Of me.

Gliding across tight stings.
A song, like the bellow of a horn,

pulled from my heart,
from the deep seat of my soul.

As if all that I feel would swallow me,
overwhelming me like a tidal wave.

WHEN I FIRST WAKE

it's dark outside.

I hear
the jangle
of the doorknob,

the creak of the hinges,

a hushed movement,
opening and closing.

The door is shut.

My sister Emma is home.
She tumbles into her bed.

⌐I HOPE FOR QUIET⌐

The silence of
a gentle snore.

But I worry — I'm
always worried.

Will I need to guard our things?

Hold her when she's crashing down?

If I'm lucky, she'll go straight
to sleep

      and I can go to school.

EMMA

Before the drugs,
before her addiction,

she was *my sister*:
        fun-loving
        hopeful
        idealistic
        loved deeply
        the big dreamer
        head in the clouds
        always reaching for more
        a romantic.

She was close
        to Mom
        to me

        to everyone.

⸙EMMA HELD MY SECRETS⸙

Comforted my fears.

Until our father got sick.
Lung cancer
ate him up.

No one knew
how to handle
the helplessness.

Mom worked more.
I played violin more.
Emma dated more,
partied harder.

That's how things started.

I THINK IT WAS A BOY

she was seeing at the time.
One of them.
The one who introduced
her to the drug.

A sip of a beer,
a puff of a joint,
a snort of a line.

From cocaine to meth.
Mom ignored the signs.
Turned away as if
nothing was happening.

AND THE DARKNESS GREW

Now we move
around each other.

Mom and I.

Like in that Greek myth.
We're Phobos and Deimos,
tiptoeing around the

God of War.

As if our whole world
would shatter
with one false
move.

LEAVING FOR SCHOOL

I can see the first
light of morning.

Pink-stained baby
blue, a touch of purple.

I peak into Emma's room.
She's asleep.

My socks are inside out.
T-shirt on backwards.

I can't remember if
        I grabbed
            my clean jeans

    or the dirty ones.

⛬IT IS THE END⛬

of December.

The seat of my bike
        is cold
        and hard, still
frosted from the night.

A gentle wind
caresses my cheeks,

rustles my hair.
I can smell the saliva

on my chapped lips.

⚬THIS IS MY ROUTINE⚬

Every morning before dawn,

I roll out of bed.

Throw on some clothes.

Ride my bike to school.

I have a zero period, an
hour before school, a

mandatory gym
class.

Punishment for ditching school
        too many times.

MOM WAS LIVID

when she got the news.

Even though she knew why.
Because of Emma.

"Aye dios mio, mija," she said.
"You will lose your scholarship."

Her words
      are camped out
      inside my brain

under perfectly
pitched tents.

AND I CAN'T COMPLAIN

because I love art school.

I begged for months to go.
I won the scholarship.

Money awarded
to only two students
every four years.

And because
if my scholarship
is canceled,

I can't afford
to attend.

SO HERE I AM

with bed-head hair
and crusty eyes.

At seven o'clock in the morning,
        more or less.

It doesn't take long
for me to change into
my PE clothes,

a color palette
of school spirit:

        blue shorts,
        white T-shirt
        with a musical
        note and the words:
        *Capella High School
        for the Arts.*

↜I DON'T FEEL FULLY AWAKE↝

until I'm sitting at my
usual spot on the bench.

Sports are not my thing.
I'm not alone in this here.
It's an art school —
sports are a punishment.

Volleyball isn't my least
favorite sport, but it's far worse
during zero period.

I sit as quietly as possible,
                    hoping

          if I slouch in just
          the right way,
          if I breathe without sound,
          if I keep my head down,
          eyes to myself, I'll be
                    invisible.

I AM

comfortable
in my solitude.

I wasn't always
a loner.
I had friends
at my other school.
But I was alone
in a different way.

At my other school,
I was Faith Navarro:
      the girl from around
      the corner.

      The girl with a mother
      who works too much.

      The girl with the
      crazy older sister.

          I am, was…

⸙ THE GIRL NOBODY KNEW ⸙

played the violin.

Yet, at the same time —
the girl who
    played some instrument
            really good.

And I *am* really good.
Proven by the countless
living room performances
for neighbors and Mom's friends.

            I was, am…

HERE

at this school,

I'm still that girl. Unknown.
I am Faith Navarro. A violinist
        in a hall full of violinists.
In classrooms full of other musicians.
In a school full of other
        really good artists.

Better artists.

I'm also really good at being invisible.

⌐SO, WHEN COACH CALLS MY NAME↝

I'm surprised. Shocked even.

I look up, dumbfounded.

Pointing at myself:
Are you sure?

"I'm not talking to myself,
Navarro," Coach says. "Up. Now."
She points to the court.

I leave the bench slowly. Every step is
as unsure as the last one.

ꝏ ANOTHER PLAYER ꝏ

throws me the ball.

It's my turn to serve.

I feel as if there is no
more air to breathe.

As if only thick
fog surrounds me.

When I arrive at the end line,
sweat drips down my face,
my neck.

I can't hear anything.
Only the sound of my
      heart
         thumping
     in my
        chest.

I THROW THE BALL

up into the air and swing
with my other hand. I miss.

I'm too nervous to look
at anyone. But all eyes
are on me.

A sea of
very annoyed eyes.

Another ball is thrown at me.
I dread trying again.

But then the blaring tone
of the bell silences the room.

I hear my name
over the intercom.

⚮SOMETIMES I WONDER⚮

what it would be like

to be in a space suit
high above Earth.

No sound. No gravity.

Only the darkness of
space. For a moment,

as I walk away
from the rest

of my PE class, I feel
awkward, bulky, floating

toward the door,
and all is silent,   unmoving.

⸎ WHEN I WALK OUT ⸎

into the hallway, I feel a rush of
cool wind.

The sound of taunting
ohs behind me.
Instantly, I am both

relieved and worried.

The one thing I am sure of is
Vice Principal Bernant's sole

purpose at Capella High—
fixing the problem kids.

᎒EVEN AN ART SCHOOL᎒

which Mom says costs an
"arm and a leg" to attend,
has its own set of troublemakers.

Stinks that I'm one of them.

I don't mean to be, you know —
a troublemaker, a problem kid.

But the other day, I ditched
school again.

Mom's going to be angry.

I TAKE MY TIME

walking to Mr. Bernant's
office.

My body is still warm
from volleyball.

My armpits tingle
with sweat.

I usually shower
after zero period.
I'm sure I smell
of BO
and morning breath.

No matter how slow
I move, I reach the
office faster than
I want.

I NEVER REMEMBER

the secretary's name.

She knows mine.
She greets me
at the entrance and
guides me to a chair
outside of Mr. Bernant's door.

I'm not sitting for long
when his door opens.

Mr. Bernant is a big,
burly man with lots
of hair. It's kind
of gross.

"Come in, Miss Navarro."

WHEN I WALK IN

there are two others.

Mrs. Cardona, my
art history teacher.
And Miss Edna, my
English lit teacher.

"What's going on?" I ask.
Anger colors my tone.

Before I can stop myself,
questions fly
out of my mouth:

"Is this an ambush?
        Am I losing my scholarship?
Are you kicking me out of school?
        Can't I explain?"

"Calm down, Faith," says Miss Edna.
"We're just here to talk."

I wonder
about what?

MR. BERNANT WARNED ME

No more absences. He warned
my mother, too.

"My last absence was excused," I say.

My cheeks redden. I avoid
looking at Mr. Bernant.

"I've already spoken to your mother," he says.

The room falls awkwardly silent.
My teachers trade glances.

"We know about your sister,"
        Mr. Bernant continues.
"We know she has a drug problem."

I don't know what to say or how
to react. I am stunned. Angry.
Ready to walk away. Ready to forget
everything. The scholarship and
this stupid school.

PITY

"What the heck is this?"

I ask.
"What does this have to do with me?"

Mr. Bernant and my teachers
look at each other again
with sorrowful eyes.
Pity.

I've never heard it said out loud.

The words linger in the air —
                an accusation
                a shame
a truth.

My sister is a drug addict.

"This is none of your business," I say.

MR. BERNANT SAYS

"I want to help you, Faith.
I'll give it to you straight.
You don't have much
of a choice here.
I know the note
you gave the office
was forged.

I should expel
you from this school.
Do you understand?
That's more than just
losing your scholarship.
You won't be able to come back.
Is that truly what you want?"

⌐I'M SO ANGRY⌐

and scared and unsure.

I can't stop
the tears.

Mrs. Cardona touches
my shoulder, and I yank
it away from her.

I can't escape. I can't walk out.

All I can do is sob. I cover my face,
and they let me cry. Until I finally say,

"Please don't hurt my family."

What I mean is:
Don't take me away.
Don't take Emma away.
Don't get authorities involved.

"We just want to help you," Miss Edna says.

Now, I look up at her, at all of them.
And I don't trust them. Because it's
never the help that is needed.
Like with my father, who died anyway.

A NEW PROGRAM

Mr. Bernant
hands me
a piece of paper.
I roll my eyes.

"You're kidding me."

"No," Mr. Bernant says.
"It's mandatory
as part of your probation
here."

The paper says in big bold letters:

The Dragons Club.
Teen-Speak Support Group.

╒═TEEN-SPEAK GROUP═╕

meets every Tuesday
at 3:45 sharp.

I walk into the cold
auditorium.

It smells of
cheap cologne
band-geek saliva
ballerina sweat.

The thud of my shoes
makes my entrance
louder than I hoped.

From the others,
a cool hi
a silent nod
a deadened stare.

From me, just a mouth
too awkward
for words.

A LARGE OPEN SPACE

Seats folded.
Curtains drawn.

We sit around each other in a circle.

The teacher enters,
wearing only white.

White cowboy boots,
white cowboy hat,
white suit.

"My name is Mr. Padilla,
but everyone calls me Boots," he says.
"I lost my father to drugs."

THERE ARE FIVE OF US

Olivia sits to the right of me.
She's an only child raised by
an aunt who is in and out of
rehab.

Finn is the tallest. He sits
        across from me.
There's an old bruise on his forearm.
        The latest fight
        with an alcoholic
        father.

Rodrigo's mom
battles heroin.

Beth, a single mother, only 16.
Her mother was an alcoholic.
Now she's dead.

And then there's me.

ꙮ *SAY SOMETHING* ꙮ

I think.

I glance at everyone,
    and then look away
nervously.

Finally, I say,
        "My name is Faith."

But it is not enough.

Mr. Padilla — Boots — he
urges me
with a single look.
Say more.

  I breathe in deeply.
        Say quickly,

"My sister is an addict. Meth."

⟡ MY WORDS ESCAPE ME ⟡

Each syllable bounces
on the auditorium walls.
    The sentence echoes
from floor to ceiling,
      from wall to wall.

It was one thing hearing others say their truth.
But now I hear my voice:
        distant, muted.

There is nothing left
for me to say in the moment.

Silence fills the room.

And my words are drowned
by the quiet spaces between us.

⌒ INTRODUCTIONS ⌒

took only five minutes.

Now Boots wants to dig deeper.
He takes out a small
wood-carved boot and holds it up.
"My father made this," he says. "He made
it in prison. He died of an overdose
shortly after giving it to me."
He pauses. "Any questions?" he says.

"Why Dragons Club?" Olivia asks.

"Good question.
What does it mean to be a dragon?
For me, it means the weight of trauma, pain,
addiction —
all that hurt is balled up into a fire ready to burn.
It gives me the strength to destroy.
But also the strength to overcome, and
the strength to heal.
For you?
It's whatever you need it to mean."

OLIVIA

"My mom died when I was four,"
Olivia says. "Dad before that."
She looks at her fresh-manicured
nails and seems uninterested
in the club.

Her Fendi backpack
sits by her feet.

She sighs, close-lipped, pink
lip gloss shining under
the light.
Says, "I live with my aunt."

Her back is straight and formal.
She speaks at a sophisticated volume —
tone flat. "She's been sober for
sixty-one days."

FINN

reveals more bruises when
he pulls a sleeve up. Fresh ones.

He catches my eyes and knows
I notice, so he pulls his sleeve down
and then slouches more in his chair.

His voice is low, quiet, and scratchy.
"I'm not sure what else to add."
He shrugs. "I guess Dad started
drinking a couple of years ago.
After—" He stops himself.
"I don't know why."

 RODRIGO

scratches his head.

Paint splatters dot his
hands like the holes in his shirt.
Paint stains his jeans.

He looks lost for words, cheeks sunken,
dark circles under his eyes.

"Right. My turn." He rakes his fingers
through his hair. "My mother
is a heroin addict. My grandpa pays
our rent, my school."

BETH

shows us a picture of her daughter.
"This is my baby," she says with pride.

Her kid has a toothy smile smushed between
chubby one-year-old cheeks.

"She has my mother's smile." Tears well
up in her eyes. "Sorry, this is still very hard
for me. My mother is an alcoholic. Was an
alcoholic. Died six months ago.
I almost left school. You know, it was too hard.
But now I live with my older sister."

FAITH

My heart thumps wildly.
"I'm a violinist. I'm here on a
scholarship. I live with my mom
and sister. Dad's dead.
My mom works
  a lot. I've missed a lot
of school…because
        of my — um, because…"

And I don't have the words.
I stand there awkwardly,
my face hot.

"Because there's no one else," Olivia says, for me.

"Because who will take care of your sister?" Rodrigo
says.

I nod and exhale.

⚡WE STAND TOGETHER⚡

at the end of our first day.

The Dragons Club gathers
in a circle, and we hold hands
while Boots leads us
in something that sounds
like a prayer.

"Basically," Boots says, "believer or nonbeliever,
this is a mantra—a way to live your life moving
forward."

Serenity—a reminder, a mantra, maybe a prayer
            of things
we cannot change and the things
we can.

            To grant us the wisdom to understand
                  the difference.

AND SOME UNICORNS, TOO

Someone wrote those words
with a purple pen
on the flyer taped to the door
that says, "Only Dragons Allowed."

As I walk past the sign, I notice
the shimmer of purple ink.

I leave the auditorium
feeling strange, as if
the world has changed,
as if the air is new.

⚘I'M NOT OBLIVIOUS⚘

to the social
structure of my
school.

Like any high school,
there is a certain order
to the in
and
out crowds.

And the inbetweeners.
Most kids here have some form
of money, from somewhere.
Capella is not cheap.

The first week, the Dragons Club kids
walk around each other like
it's a secret.

Good thing
I'm used to keeping secrets.

⋲IN OUR SECOND MEETING⋺

Boots jumps right in
with a story about his dad.

Breaks the ice for us.

"He used to take me fishing.
That's how it was when things
were level. He was a good dad
and great at fishing.
When I was younger, I'd feel sad
about those times because of how
unfair it was when he was on drugs.
But now I cherish them.

I think that's important.
Remembering the good.
Taking inspiration where you
can find it.

What is something that inspires you
about someone you love?"

⁓WE BEGIN⁓

Olivia sits with her arms and legs
crossed. She is the first to talk.
"My aunt used to be a model.
She's really amazing."

"*You* could be a model," Rodrigo says.
He smiles. Olivia rolls her eyes.

"I'm an artist, so that's not weird to say,"
Rodrigo says in his defense.
He continues:

"My grandfather is an artist, too. Painter."
Rodrigo's bangs are so long, they dip in
front of his eyes. He flips his head to move
his hair out of the way. "He studied in France."

I try not to roll *my* eyes.

⸮A CARROT-EATING ONE-YEAR-OLD⸮

appears on Beth's phone.

"My daughter, Lilyanna." She clarifies this,
as if we don't know. "I named her
after my great-grandmother, a ballerina.
Her legacy encouraged me to keep performing,
even after I got pregnant."

My own voice shocks me
as I respond. "My sister—Emma—
she encouraged me to play the violin."
I'm surprised at the ease of my words.
"It was hard to learn at first.
But she made me keep going."

Finn is quieter than the rest of us.
"My mom used to be an actress."

BETH IS LIKE RODRIGO

They both blend
into the crowd
quite easily.

Known and not known.
A regular
they-seem-nice
type.

I see them in English lit.
Both wave at me, cheerfully.

And suddenly, I have friends.

I wave back with a smile.

FINN IS ALWAYS ALONE

He almost blends into the lockers
        and bookshelves.
        Quiet. Reserved.

We don't have any classes
        together. But I
        see him in the hall.

He has earbuds in and
looks to the ground.

I think he sees me, and I smile,
but he looks through me.

As if he's a ghost, or maybe I am.

OLIVIA IS POPULAR

but distant.

I notice her more
now, since we started
the Club. I wonder
if her other friends
know about her aunt.
Like, know the whole
story or part of it.

Does she keep it secret,
the way I hide my sister?

I expected her to be like Finn.
But in orchestra, she says hi
with her clarinet in one hand,
her backpack in the other.

⌐ THE AUDITORIUM IS
EXTRA COLD ⌐

when we meet again.

I walk in a few minutes late.
The mood is different.
Beth is there with Lilyanna,
holding the baby
in her lap.

Rodrigo is on his phone.

Finn slumps over with his forearms
on his knees, looking at the ground.

Boots and Olivia are off to the side
having a serious conversation.
When they come back to the circle,
it's clear Olivia has been crying.

"Only if you want to," Boots says
to Olivia.

She nods.

IT'S THE FIRST TIME

Olivia shows she cares.

Her eyes are red and still teary.
Everyone is staring at her, but
she sits there quietly.

"Are you okay?" asks Rodrigo.

Olivia looks up at him and then
at all of us. More tears well up,
out of her control.

"My aunt started drinking again."
She sobs suddenly and then stops.
She takes a deep breath. "I'm fine."

BETH SAYS

"I don't think you're fine."

Olivia snaps back.
"How would you know?"

Beth looks confused.
"We all know. That's the point."

"No. *Your* mom drank herself to death.
My aunt is just—"

Boots interjects, "Beth means
we understand because we—
the Club—are going or have gone
through it, too.
That's why we're here."

⟡ OLIVIA RETURNS ⟡

to her *normal*. Polite. Formal.

"I apologize.
I didn't mean it that way."

"Our situations feel isolating,"
Boots says. "You feel like no one
else in the world can understand.
That's why this group is important."

Beth's face is still flushed red,
but she nods in acceptance.

BETH CONFESSES

"I felt that way whenever Mom
went on a binge. Worried that
she'd end up dead."

"Me too," says Boots. "And
when the day came—"

"—it was the worst." Beth pauses.
She's hesitant but continues, "But
we're okay now." She turns red.

"—Because it's come to an end,"
says Boots.

We're quiet then.
Because we all know
what it feels like
to watch someone slowly
kill themselves.

⚘AN INVITATION⚘

arrives in my school email
on Saturday.

The subject line says:
*Dragons and Unicorns,
A Meet-Up.*

I'm surprised. Especially
after the last meeting.

Olivia is inviting
the group to her house
for a get-together. I look
up the address. She lives
in one of the richest
areas in the city.

SATURDAY MORNING, I WAKE

I settle on a
hand-me-down
red dress.

My brown hair hangs
long. Straight
with large, loopy curls
at the bottom.

 I don't wear
 a lot of makeup.

Just mascara
and a touch
of lip gloss.

Ready early, I decide
to practice violin.

IN FRONT OF THE MIRROR

I hold my violin.
The case is open
on a stool
next to me.

I run the resin
on the bow and
place it back
in its case.

Lifting my instrument
to my chin, resting
the black cradle
against my skin.
The woodsy scent
of the violin
energizes me.

I slide the bow
over the strings,
slowly at first.

♪THE SONG♪

weaves together
the sound, the
bow, the
strings, me.

All fluid, separate
but together,
all at once.

And I am lifted.

I exist outside
of this place,
my home and school
and the world.

I'm high above
Earth, above
the atmosphere,
where poets dream
of the stars.

⚜ WHEN THE SONG ENDS ⚜

satisfaction
washes over me.

A completion
hard to explain.

As I'm putting
my violin away,
I hear the door
open and shut.

"Mom," I call out.
I note the time
on the clock.

Mom is probably
at work. Which
means my sister
is home early.

Dread fills my stomach.

OUTSIDE OF MY ROOM

Emma is making a ruckus.

I go into the hallway
and see her looking
through the hall
closet.

She's taking out
all of the storage
containers,
looking for
something.

She looks up at me,
and I catch her eyes.

I can see the meth
in her pupils,
the way they're
bigger in the light.

THE WAY EMMA IS

is so different from who she was.

Like she's far away,
her body
only a shell.

Like a ghost,
she exists
outside of time,
and so do I.

She's the thinnest
I've ever seen, a
skeleton dancing
on an altar. Not a
guard but a
warning
between
worlds.

EMMA ASKS FOR MONEY

after searching
through the hall closet
and finding nothing.

I tell her I don't have any.
She looks at me
as if she doesn't
believe me.

We fight over this often,
when she takes and sells
what she can.

I can feel my anger
migrate from my
chest to my fingertips.
I see her eyes
drift toward my violin.

EMMA LIES AND STEALS

and then lies about stealing.

She's worse
when the high
of meth is gone.
All depression and tears.

I shove my violin
under my pillow.
Guarding it
like a dragon.

When she's like *this*,
there's no stopping her,
and I don't want to fight.

I remember the old
coffee can under my
bed stuffed with cash
collected over the
months since my
birthday.

ᝰ EMMA REMEMBERS ᝰ

the coffee can, too.

Without asking, she
reaches under my
bed and grabs it.

"That's mine," I say.
My protest is useless.

Emma says,
"It's for my friend.
He's having car trouble
and needs to get home."

~EMMA LOOKS AT ME~

with her blank eyes.

I know she's lying,
but I give it to her
anyway.

Because if
I don't, there
will be *tears*.

Because she'll take it anyway.
Because I don't want to miss the
party to babysit her when
the low kicks in.

Because sometimes it feels
like when she doesn't steal
my violin, she's saying
she still loves me.

ALONE IN MY ROOM

I cry.

I'm sad and angry
and hurt. But I'm mostly
mad at myself.

I am selfish
for not wanting to give it to her,

and

I am selfish for giving
it to her anyway.

And I feel the guilt—because
I gave her the money so I can
see my friends.

I feel the guilt and go anyway.

✦I ARRIVE AT OLIVIA'S✦

a few minutes late.

Everyone is already
there.

I want to tell them
about my sister but
decide against it.

Out of anyone, this group
would understand.

But even Finn is there,
and he's actually smiling.

I don't want to ruin
the mood. So, I join
them and forget.

OLIVIA'S AUNT

is at rehab.

"She'll be there
for a while."

"You're here
by yourself?"
Rodrigo asks.

Olivia shrugs.
"Pretty much.
The maid is here."

"She's not your
guardian though,"
Beth says.

"I'm fine," Olivia says.

We all know
she's not.

⚘ WE PLAY MONOPOLY ⚘

and drink flavored seltzers.

We talk about everything not
school related and definitely
nothing about the Club.

Finn seems more alive today, and
he looks nice when he smiles.

Beth counts her money and
properties. Rodrigo and Olivia
are lost in their own
conversation.

We leave for home
late at night.

⌁THE DRAGONS CLUB CREW⌁

The five of us meet once
a week in school and most
weekends.

We feel normal together.
Nothing hidden, and nothing
to be said.

In school, our club meetings
are about our feelings,
memories, boundaries.

Some weeks are heavy,
like when Beth speaks
of her mother's death.

The weekends are chill.
Board games and food.
Finn performs Shakespeare.
He's impressive. Out of his shell.

THIS WEEK

Rodrigo tells us
why his clothes
are tattered,
paint-stained,
and old.

"If I ask for new clothes,
Mom will cry
because she feels
like a bad mother.
I don't want
to give her
the reason.

What if
it's the thing
that pushes her
over the edge?"

⸙I ADD TO THE DISCUSSION⸙

which has become
a usual thing for me.

A feeling of comfort has set in.

"I don't buy
things either,"
I tell Rodrigo.

"My sister will
just steal them.

I'm lucky I
have my violin."

⟞ "I'LL BUY YOU CLOTHES" ⟝

Olivia says and laughs.

Rodrigo laughs, too.

I think Olivia is
only half-kidding.

"Boundaries!" Beth laughs.

Boots gets serious,
"Boundaries and detachment
are tough to learn.
We learn this as part
of our journey here
together."

The room is quieted.

Boot emphasizes, "We learn."

DETACHMENT AND BOUNDARIES

are not easy.

Especially in my home.
Mom worries too much.

The way Boots explains it,
I need to:

Love Emma enough
to let go. She can learn.

Love myself enough
to not take the blame and
know that I'm not the reason.

I am only responsible for *me*.

&MY ATTENDANCE RECORD&

has improved, but I'm not
sure if it's because of the Club.

My sister is still
the same,
a roller-coaster
ride.

One minute she seems *almost* okay,
the next she's animated, unusually
happy. And the next she's dramatic
and in tears and the whole world
is against her.

Mom put locks on our bedroom doors.

⟿ NEW CROWD ⟾

We spend another
Saturday together
at Olivia's.
She sees us
more than her
old crowd.

Finn is there early,
and we talk about the
upcoming school play.

It's the only time he
seems happy, bright.

Finn, like most students
here, is multitalented:

actor—writer—pianist.
He will play Amadeus.

 SURPRISE

Beth surprises us
with her voice.
In all the meetings we've had,

I never once asked what *she* does,
why she's here at Capella.

I feel like a jerk because of it.

She sings her part in the play,
her voice operatic.
It's so beautiful.

Finn recites a few lines,
and we all laugh
because when he's in character,
he's a whole different person.

I'M SITTING NEXT TO FINN

and we're closer than usual.

He's wearing a light,
sandalwood cologne.

His face is nice when he smiles.
His mood is playful when relaxed.

Beth notices us and winks
at me when I look at her.

Finn places his hand over mine,
and we smile at each other.

⸎FINN AND I⸎

hang out with each other
at school now without the others.

I help him run lines
and get into character.

I know more about why he's so quiet.
How his father is when he's drunk.

The bruises on his arms have faded.
But his hand is swollen and red.

I wonder sometimes if his silence
is the only thing holding back his anger.

FINN AND I DON'T VISIT

each other at home.

We understand each
other in this way.

To know in theory
is one thing.

To know in reality
is quite another.

And I think we're both
afraid to show
the reality of our lives.

WHEN WE KISS

nothing else exists.

Not Finn's father

or my sister. Just us.

And it's amazing and

beautiful and regular.

⚮ IT'S MARCH ⚮

Most students are involved
   with the play, the big finale,

the end-of-the-year performance.

Rodrigo is one of the painters
   creating the backdrops.

Olivia and I are in the orchestra.

Beth is acting and singing.

Finn is the lead.

LIKE A ROLLER COASTER

After the slow, steady ride up,
the hill becomes a fast drop.

And we drop—the whole
bunch of us.

Beth's baby is really sick.

Olivia's aunt is home
from rehab but drinking again.

Rodrigo's mom has disappeared,
all too common on her heroin binges.

And Finn's dad is Finn's dad.

⸓BOOTS INTERVENES⸓

after seeing Finn's black eye.

Social Services removes Finn
from his father's home.

And I worry, selfishly,
what his removal means for us.

Because without his father,
    there's no art school.

Because the state
    isn't going to pay his tuition.

⸕OLD WAYS⸎

Finn is in school
for now, but no one
has talked about
what happened.

Not even Boots.

The yellow-faded
bruise around
Finn's eye
fills the room.
He won't talk to anyone.
Not even me.

Things are so hard.

I'm tempted
to cut school.

But my scholarship
is at stake.

I don't cut, but
it's easy to see
how people slip
back into
old ways.

⸙ FRIDAY COMES ⸙

and there's a new energy
added to the mix
at Capella.

The buzz of the coming
play is in the air,
the whole school working
on a single project.

Just a few weeks to prepare.

I'm kinda excited, too.
But anxious things
will go wrong.

Anxiety
is at the core
of my depression.

I can't help but think,
I cannot prevent a crisis.

⟿MY BIKE RIDE HOME⟿

from school is like a meditation.

Like playing violin, a rhythmic
movement of the pedals.

The cars next to me blend
in with the trees. I see only
the bike path.

Like playing the violin,
it is a time of escape,
when my mind is clear.

My violin sits safely
in my backpack.

⚘AT HOME I NOTICE⚘

my mom's TV is missing.

Crystal vases, too—an anniversary
gift from my dad.

Mom is sitting
on her bed in her room

holding an emptied
jewelry box. Again.

Mom's eyes are puffy and red.
Her cheeks still wet from her tears.

I clutch my violin close.

❧TOUGH LOVE☙

is never as easy as it sounds.

Too many what-ifs.
If we lock Emma out,

  will she die?

  My mind goes
  to the worst-case scenario.

Mom has the same fears.
I say to her what I say to myself.

What I learned in the Dragons Club.
What Boots drives home in every session.

Do not suffer because of Emma's actions.

↝ MOM CHANGES ↜

the locks on the front door.

She sits me down
in the living room
and explains why.

She looks
guilty and worried
and hesitant.

Tough love is hard.

Mom is rambling on, and
I can tell she cares

what I think. I can see
the shame in her eyes.

"IT'S OKAY"

I say to my mom.

We can't cover
for Emma anymore.

We can't hide
what she does.

I squeeze my mom's
hands in mine.

"It's okay," I say again,
through her tears and my own.

⚬MY ANXIETY⚬

is even worse since
Mom changed the locks.

I wonder where Emma is,
if she's safe, alive.

I know Mom is wondering, too.
Worry seeps into every room

in the house.

MY SATURDAY PLANS

are simple.

Morning violin practice.
Then a meet-up
at Olivia's with the Club.

I'm learning
to focus on myself.

But it isn't easy. It's been two
weeks since I've seen Finn.

Olivia's aunt is home
and trying to stay sober.

⚘ STILL NO SIGN ⚘

Week three, March. No Emma.
My week is as follows:

Monday — No Emma. No Finn.

Tuesday — No Emma. No Finn.
   The Dragons Club @ 3:45 — No Finn.
(No one asks. Does Boots know anything?)

Wednesday — No Emma. No Finn.

Thursday — No Emma. No Finn.

Friday — No Emma. No Finn.

Saturday and Sunday — No one,
just me and my violin.

⟞FINN'S FATHER DIED⟝

Rodrigo read the obit
in the newspaper.

Alcohol poisoning. A binge after
Finn was removed.

The temptation to ditch
school is stronger than ever.

But I don't. Instead, I wait.

This is my life lately—waiting.

I wait for news about Emma,
about Finn.

WHEN FINN FINALLY CALLS

I'm practicing violin in
front of my mirror.

"I'm sorry I didn't
        call sooner," he says.

"I wish you had," I say.

I ask him when he will
be back in school—if

he will be back. His tuition
is paid for the month,

and then it's public school.

AN UNDERSTUDY

would come in handy
for all the days of school
I missed.

For the days I
may miss in the future.

I could send my understudy
to class or to care for my sister.

Finn's understudy
is taking over his part.

I think he's disappointed about it.

 EMMA

is two years older.

She was born in April, this month.

She listens to country and binges
Grey's Anatomy.

She laughs wholeheartedly and loves fiercely
and is annoyingly stubborn.

She can eat a whole box of Oreo
cookies in one sitting.

She is still locked out.

THE DAY I DITCH SCHOOL

Mom is at work.

She texts me
about Emma.

A neighbor saw Emma
around the house.
Mom is sure she'll break in.

It's like she's asking —without asking—
for me to make sure.

I know I shouldn't.
Will anyone notice?

After Emma left, Mom asked,
"Do you think I'm cruel?"

No was my answer.
Now I'm not sure.

﹏MY HOUSE IS EMPTY﹏

when I get there.

No one
is inside or outside.

The screen on Emma's
bedroom window is bent,

which confirms Emma
was there. I take inventory

and nothing is missing.
        I hope she's okay.

~QUESTIONS~

about Emma
run through my mind.

I worry if she is hungry or cold.
I stuff a grocery bag

with a change of clothes,
a water bottle, and an energy bar.

I place the bag on top
of the bush outside

her window.
The bag is gone in the morning.

IT'S LIKE FALLING OFF THE WAGON

The need to help
someone when you

know you shouldn't.
I leave my sister her

bag of necessities almost daily.
I can't leave the bag in the morning

because Mom might see it before she goes
to work. Or when she comes home.

HALF OF A CLASS DOESN'T COUNT

This is how I rationalize
my actions.

The last class of the day,
I show up for roll call.

Sitting in the back near
the door affords me this one perk.

I leave 15 minutes in, and I get
home on time.

⚘MY LAST CLASS⚘

of the day is math.

I always make sure to do
my homework and
turn it in before I leave.

I can follow
the book examples.

And like a math function,
my days are reduced
to input and output.

The only variation is Tuesday.
I don't skip Dragons Club.

℀OUR CLUB MEETINGS℀

aren't the same.

Finn's departure is looming.
We haven't met at Olivia's

since her aunt's latest return
from rehab. Beth only shows

up every other meeting. And
Rodrigo might move.

Maybe it's just me.

Because I'm keeping
secrets again.

⌾ THE SCHOOL PLAY ⌾

is moving forward
with or without me.

Worse, I don't even care.
Besides school, I haven't

been practicing my violin.
I haven't practiced for the play.

The bag has been like an
obsession the last few weeks.

And I know I shouldn't leave it
because it's really not helping Emma.

It's only enabling her behavior.

THE THING ABOUT SECRETS

Some eventually come to the light.

After three weeks, the worry
and what-ifs weigh on me.

What if my mom comes home
early one day?

What if I miss a test day
in math by accident?

What if a teacher catches me
leaving campus early?

Something will happen.
Eventually.

The question is,
which way will be first?

MOM COMES HOME EARLY

and sees the bag on the bush.

I know this because
I'm in my room.

She's angry when she comes
inside, holding the bag.

"Do you think I don't want to help her?"
she asks. "Do you think this is easy for me?"

⌁I YELL BACK⌁

"Do you think this is easy for *me*?"

"No," she says.
"But you're not
 helping her. Not really."

"But this is what you wanted, right?"
I say to her.
"Why else would you even tell
me what the neighbor said?
So you don't have to feel guilty."

"I already feel guilty!" she says.

TODAY IS MATH TEST DAY

and I forgot until now,
when Mom's yelling.

Double whammy.

Mom comes home early,
and I miss a test.

A phone call will follow soon.
I sit in my room and wait. Hoping

somehow my math teacher
doesn't notice my absence.

Butterflies rage in my stomach.

❧THE SCHOOL CALLS❧

later in the afternoon.

I know this because
of the way my mom
answers the phone.

"Yes, this is Faith's mom."
I overhear the conversation.
"No, I didn't know.
Thank you."

Mom says to me,
"Mrs. Cardona saw you
leaving campus the day
before yesterday."

Triple whammy.

TUESDAY AT 3:45

Dragons Club begins.
It's Finn's last meeting.
Everyone is here, finally.

Boots asks me what happened.
I don't tell him about ditching school.
But I tell him about the bag.

I worry my friends and
Boots will be disappointed
in me.

"My clothes are
full of holes," Rodrigo says.

"I used to water down
my mother's liquor," Beth says.

They know how to make me
feel less alone.

⁓ DETACHMENT ⁓

is not cruel.

Boots reminds
us of this.

He continues,
"Part of your
own recovery
is to not
allow your
sister to use
you in this way.

Don't feel guilty.
Really helping Emma means
letting her face the
consequences of
her actions."

 RECOVERY

is a weird word.

How am I in recovery?
I'm not the addict.

Then I realize I am.

Recovery is defined
as a "return to a
normal state of health,
mind, or strength."

And I am reaching
for recovery every
second Emma is
out there.

AT THE END

of the meeting,
before we leave,
Rodrigo announces
he is moving.

Rodrigo's grandfather
came for a visit, and
now he and his mom
are moving to France.

His mom will
go into rehab there.

"How soon?" I ask.

"This weekend," he says.

I'm happy and sad for him.

BETH HAS SCHEDULING CONFLICTS

"I don't want to drop the group,"
she says. "But between school,
the play, and Lilyanna…"

"And I'm graduating," Olivia says.

Finn, Rodrigo, Beth, and Olivia.
They're all leaving me.

I guess I'm the only
mandatory member.

BOOTS ASKS ME TO STAY AFTER

I linger behind,
waiting for the
auditorium to empty.

Boots asks me to sit
so we can talk. And
the raging butterflies
are back. I know what
he's going to say.

He knows I ditched school.

Is he going
to deliver
the bad news?

I START FIRST

I say, "You know."
"Yes," Boots says.

He asks, "You
know what happens next?"
"Yes," I say.

I lose my scholarship.

"I wish I had a say
in what happens,
but I don't.
I can only recommend.
And I recommended another
chance for you."

⚬ "THE CLUB IS OVER." ⚬

I say this to Boots.

"Not necessarily," he says.

I don't believe him.
There's only me left,
and my scholarship
might be gone soon.
Which means my tuition
won't be paid. And
it's back to public
school for me.

And public school
does not have
a music program.

⚜ "HAVE A LITTLE FAITH" ⚜

Boots says this to me.
Like I haven't heard *that* before.

"I'll try. I promise," I say.

He continues,

"Your name is a good
match for you.

Faith is knowing
without knowing.

It is trust.
Like knowing the sun

will always rise
after it sets."

MOM IS HOME

when I get there.

I brace myself for
what comes next.

The last we spoke,
we argued. And I
swear I don't think
she's wrong for
changing the locks.

I don't want her
to feel guilty. But
I'm mad she puts
everything on me.

WHEN WE TALK

this time, there is no yelling.

Mom seems to make an
actual attempt to listen
to me. I tell her I don't blame her.

I never have. And she is relieved.
But when she avoids Emma,

I always end up skipping school
to pick up the pieces.

MOM SHOWS ME THE LETTER

"They didn't waste
any time," I say.

"Do you want me to open it
with you?" she asks.

"No," I say. "If you don't mind.
I'd rather open it alone."

THE LETTER

It's stuffed into an off-white,
parchment-looking envelope.

Capella High School for the Arts

is on the upper right corner in big
bold letters in a fancy font.

My heartbeat thumps heavily.
I feel it in my fingertips.

I cannot wait. I rip
the envelope open.

⚬IT'S OFFICIAL⚬

The letter is short and to the point.

My scholarship is void due to an
unsatisfactory attendance record.

Is it possible to die from heartache?
Everything I've worked for is gone.

I can't stop the tears from coming.
I sob until I'm out of breath, until I sleep.

⤷I ATTEND MY LAST⤶

days at Capella High.

I eat lunch
with Beth and Rodrigo.

Hang out with
Olivia in the halls

before orchestra. And
meet with Finn after school

for about an hour.
I'm not grounded, luckily.

Mom figures I got the worst
kind of consequence:

losing my scholarship.

᚛I GET A PHONE CALL᚜

from Emma.

She asks for food.
If I can let her in to shower.

My mind begins to spiral into a wide
variety of what-ifs. I remember

what Boots said: *Do not suffer*.
I am only responsible for myself.

"No," I say.

MY LAST DAY AT CAPELLA

I'm finishing
zero period when

I get a text.

Emma is in the hospital.

This is my biggest fear. I can feel
the vein pulse in my neck.

I hop on my bike and, with
wobbly knees, ride as fast

as I can to the hospital.

⌓I ARRIVE AT
THE HOSPITAL⌓

and ask the receptionist
for my sister's room.

She's on the fourth floor,
critical care unit.

Emma is not conscious and
looks frail, like she hasn't

had a meal in a while.
Her chart says 90 pounds.

Her room is dark, lit only
by the hall light.

AFTER A FEW HOURS

my mom arrives.

I'm sitting in
a chair watching
the IV solution
drip in its bag.

"How's she doing?"
Mom asks. I shrug.

Emma is still asleep.

Her room smells like
rubbing alcohol.
The beeping of the EKG
echoes in the room.

Uneaten food sits on a
tray near her bed.

ᚔEMMA'S HEARTᚔ

is damaged.

Hypertension. Malnutrition.
Severe dehydration.

She's lucky to be alive. But we're not
out of the woods yet.

Someone brought Emma
to the hospital. A friend and

fellow addict. They stuck
around long enough to give

the triage nurse Emma's name
and contact information.

⸺FOUR DAYS⸺

are spent at the hospital, mostly.

Mom and I take turns going home
to rest, shower, eat, and change.

When Emma finally wakes,
I get the news from my mom.

She sends a text to my phone.
I grab a cold Pop Tart and head

over to the hospital right away.

I RIDE MY BIKE

to the hospital.

I hesitate before going
into the elevator.

I'm sad and afraid,
but mostly angry.

I'm tired, and
I'm going to tell her.

WHEN I REACH THE FOURTH FLOOR

the elevator door dings.

My palms are sweaty,
and my armpits sting.

A one-person intervention.

I finally realize now,
this is the boundary.

⟡AN INTERVENTION⟡

is when one or more people
confront an addict with their addiction.

Then they ask that the addict go
into rehab. It is meant to be

a frank and open discussion.
Total and complete honesty.

When I walk into my sister's
room, I'm ready. The whole

world melts away.

⚘I SAY IT FAST⚘

"Emma, I love you,
but I can't suffer any longer.

Neither can Mom. You have a
drug problem. You are an addict.

And it's hurting—it's hurting
your family. We want you to get help.

Please.

I found one free rehab through
the city, and two low-cost programs."

I hold out the three pamphlets
I have in my hand.

⸎THE ROOM IS SILENT⸎

after my words.

Mom is staring
at the pamphlets in my hand.

Slowly, she reaches for them.
I give them to her. She flips

through them. Emma sniffles softly.
I see her reflection in the window.

She doesn't just look sickly.
She looks aged, worn.

WHEN THE CRYING STOPS

the sun begins to set.

The brilliant orange hue
scatters across the room.

It gives a magical glow
to the white linens that cover my sister.

Emma has a choice in front of her.

I stare at her
until she looks at me
eye-to-eye.

She agrees.

EMMA IS GOING TO REHAB

and I'm happy.

Mom is happy
but cautious.

I know how this can go.

Emma can flake.

Or go and not get better.

Or get better and then fall
right back into her drugs.

Like Rodrigo's mom and
Olivia's aunt.

But Mom and I are
hopeful.

↩MY SISTER↪

leaves the hospital.

She checks in with a
low-cost program.

A sliding scale Mom can afford.
She'll live there for a few weeks.

There she'll get counseling
and drug counseling.

She'll be fed and looked after.
She'll be safe there.

EMMA'S 12 STEPS

begin with an apology to Mom
and then to me.

She writes a letter
to my school.

It's a long shot, but she hopes
they will give me another chance.

I hope so, too.
But with a heavy
dose of reality.

It will hurt less if it's a no.

I ENROLL IN
PUBLIC SCHOOL

Even though there's only
a few weeks or so left.

I'm disappointed
but want to make the best of it.

Mom encourages me to play violin.
She tells me to keep practicing, and I do.

I wear a pink shirt, blue jeans,
and tennis shoes on the first day.

Keep telling myself,
Stay positive and don't give up.

RETURNING TO MY OLD SCHOOL

is like coming home
after summer camp.

The school isn't as
nice and new as
Capella High.

The entire school is
wrapped in a 10-foot-tall,
chain-link fence.

Metal detectors at every entrance.
More like a prison than a school.

I ride my bike and enter
through the back.

SEEING MY OLD FRIENDS

is nice though. I get a lot of
"What the heck happened to you?"

I shrug and don't explain. The letter
from Capella High still stings.

It's like being rejected but worse.

Some of my classmates here
never knew I left in the first place.

⌒I WONDER⌒

about the school play.

Capella's
end-of-the-year finale.

I wish I could,
at the very least, see the
performance.

It stinks I won't
be a part of it.

I check out the
school website.

I TALK TO MY NEW-OLD PRINCIPAL

about a music program.
Why can't we have one?

And if they would ever consider it.
He said the school doesn't have the

budget for an arts or music
program. He wishes it was different.

Art and music are important subjects,
just as important as math and English.

I PLAY VIOLIN

in my room after school.

The first slide of the bow
makes a rich, deep sound.

Like a whistle —formal
and proud. I dive into

Vivaldi, a violin concerto
in A minor.

Lighter in mood
and the song helps me.

In this space,
nothing can hurt me.

MOM IS HAPPIER

Emma is doing well in rehab.
And though I'm not at Capella,

I'm playing my violin, going to school,
and hanging out with old friends.

Life seems better in a way.
I am grateful.

When worries creep in,
I ride my bike or play my violin.

I focus on myself.

⸙ THERE'S A KNOCK ⸙

at my front door.

It's Boots.

"Hi?" I say. Confusion
riddles my face. Mom comes
up behind me. The meeting
was prearranged. I know by
how my mom greets him.
She's not surprised.

"Come in," Mom says.
"How are you?"

"Fine," Boots says.

HOW MUCH MORE TROUBLE

could I be in?

Does Capella want to
ban me for life?

Tell me to stop playing
violin?

I think my face
wears my worry.

Boots smiles gently.

"You're not in trouble,"
he says. "But I am here
about your scholarship."

⚔ MY SCHOLARSHIP ⚔

is being reinstated.

And I can't believe my ears.

Boots's recommendation along
with my sister's letter

convinced Mr. Bernant
to give me another chance.

I'm stunned.

"Really?!" I ask.

"Yes, really."

I jump up and down,

screaming a good
kind of scream.

Crying a good
kind of cry.

~ SECOND CHANCES ~

or a third in my case,
aren't to be taken for granted.

"Don't blow it this time,"
Boots says, seriously.
"Remember what I always say
to the Dragons?"

I nod.

"Focus on myself," I say.
"Like you taught us.

Don't be used. Don't suffer.
Detachment is not cruel.

I can love my sister and
still have boundaries."

⤜BOOTS LEAVES IN STYLE⤚

"Boots is a nice man," Mom says
after he's gone. "Does he always wear that?"

      "Yes, and a matching cowboy hat."

"Never anything else?"

      "Nope."

I'm looking down at what
he's left me—
his wooden boot,
the one his father made him.

"He spoke to me
about your club," Mom says.
"You know, Faith, I'm sorry, too.
All of the pressure I've put on you.
I want you to focus
on yourself like you said."

I promise her—and myself—
that I will.

MOM COOKS

my favorite dinner.

Homemade macaroni and cheese,
extra cheesy.

I think she's feeling guilty,
but this time because of me.

I wonder what she and Boots talked about.
It must have been some conversation.

I'LL BE BACK AT CAPELLA

next week.

I'll finish the rest of this week
at public school.

Olivia and Beth text me their
yays and congratulations.

It feels unreal to me.

My fear sneaks in when I'm
not looking. The anxiety.

Like if I breathe the wrong way,
I'll lose my scholarship all over again.

IN THE MORNING

I'm up before dawn.

My body's clock is still tuned
into my zero period.

My last day at public
school is uneventful. And I enjoy

the calm, the serenity of what I
can control: me.

It is the Dragons'
mantra, a prayer.

SUNDAY NIGHT BEFORE SCHOOL

is the night before Emma
comes home.

Anxiety hums in every cell of my body.

Sometimes I feel like the latest
events are just a dream.

Like I'll wake any moment
and my sister will be an addict

on the streets. My scholarship
will still be null and void.

Life without my violin.

MY FIRST DAY BACK AT CAPELLA

Monday, after zero period,
Olivia and Beth meet me
at the front of the school.

We hug and laugh
and our smiles are brighter
than the sun.

"Just in time for the play," Beth says.

"Are they giving you back your seat?"
asks Olivia.

"No," I say.

MY SEAT IN
THE ORCHESTRA

has shifted to second
violin section.

But I'm no longer seated
for the play.

I'm bummed out but
understand why my chair
was given to a different violinist.

At lunch, I buy my ticket
for the play: *Amadeus*.

THE NEXT DAY IN ZERO PERIOD

I'm called to the vice principal's
office again.

It's only the second
time, but it feels like a habit.

Mr. Bernant is sitting at his desk
when I walk in.

A fresh bowl of crushed flowers
sits in one corner,

filling the room
with a floral scent.

MR. BERNANT'S CONDITIONS

are simple.

Summer school
to make up for the days
I missed.

Zero period until
I graduate.

And no more absences.

Come hell or high water.
Come rain or shine.
I cannot miss one day.

Nothing short of death
will excuse me.

"Got it?" Mr. Bernant asks.

"Got it," I say.

⚘ BEFORE I LEAVE ⚘

Mr. Bernant's office, he stops me
at the door.

"Faith," he says. "You
have a lot of potential.

I'm not saying this so you'll feel bad,
but instead to inspire you.

You could have been first chair. But
sometimes talent isn't enough."

I NOD, NOT SAYING ANYTHING

I'm grateful
for my scholarship.

I'm grateful for the chance
I have now.

First chair would have been amazing!

And I won't lie, the news stings.
But violin is a part of me.

Part of my soul.
Playing is a privilege.

I play with or without Capella.

IN THE AUDITORIUM

No Finn. No Rodrigo.
But Olivia and Beth are there.

"Come in, Faith," Boots says.
I greet the others with a smile.

"I thought you two weren't
coming to the club anymore," I say.

They just smile at me. Boots says,
"The Dragons Club will break for the summer.

We will start again next year, Faith.
But with a new group."

I'M ALWAYS NERVOUS

around new people.

But I felt like that
when the club began.

And now I can't imagine
this last year without

Olivia or Beth,

without Rodrigo
or Finn.

⚡OUR LAST MEETING⚡

is like the ones before.

We talk about our lives:

regular things and stuff
that hurts.

Boots asks
how Emma is doing.

"Good," I say. "She's coming home today."

"Are you okay?" he asks.

⚞ I'M SCARED ⚟

is my first thought. I hesitate.

"Anxious," Boots says.

"Like it's going to be the same old mess," Olivia says. "I know how that is."

I nod. "Yeah. To put it lightly. But I have faith." I smile.

"Is your aunt still sober?" I ask. Olivia nods.

OLIVIA'S AUNT

Her sobriety gives me hope.

Emma's problem is different,
but maybe she won't relapse.

I've heard of that happening,
rehab working the first time.

Emma wants to change.
She wants to get better,

do better. I hope it is enough.
I pray for Emma.

ON MY WAY HOME

I stop at a nearby park.

I watch the little kids play
on the monkey bars and swings.

When I was little, lying on the
swing on my belly was my thing.

Emma would twist the swing
for me really tight and let go.

And I'd twirl with the seat
round and round and round.

I always had faith
that she had my back.

⌒JUST STAY FOCUSED⌒

There's not much else I can do.
I can worry. My anxiety

can fry my brain, sap my
energy, and drag me down.

Or I can set worry aside,
place it in a box,

and push it
away.

Focus on myself.

That is all I can ever control in this life.

EMMA IS HOME

when I get there.

She's in the kitchen
with Mom preparing dinner.

Mom is prepping a whole chicken.
Emma is cutting the green beans.

She smiles at me
when I walk into the kitchen.

"Welcome home," Mom says.
"Want to peel potatoes?"

"Sure," I say.

DINNER IS DELICIOUS

and Emma looks healthier.

Her eyes are alive and kind.
Her body is thin but not as bony.

A stark contrast to her
appearance at the hospital.

We are happy
in this moment,
and I savor it.

I crunch into a green bean.

I enjoy the *now*.

⟿ STAYING PRESENT ⟿

is one of the tasks I work on.

Not regretting the past.
Not worrying about the future.

When my thoughts stray,
I interrupt them and bring myself

back to the present, to where
I am existing now.

And I breathe deeply.

ANOTHER LETTER

arrives in the mail.

The same official off-white,
and the same fancy letters

in script:
Capella High School for the Arts.

It's my official
reinstatement letter.

I already started school again,
but I'm happy to see the actual letter.

Tears well up in my eyes, and
in an instant they fall.

Seeing the official letter is like a release,
as if all of the pressure built up

inside of me lets go.

THE UNCERTAINTY
OF A RELAPSE

lingers somewhere
in the back of my mind.

But I try not to dwell on it.
The possibility is always there,

but *I will not create a crisis*
where there isn't one.

I repeat that often.

⚘ AMADEUS ⚘

is a smash.

I stand with the
others and clap—a
standing ovation.

I'm so proud of Beth.
She rocked her part.
Olivia and the rest
of the orchestra were
fantastic.

"Next year," Emma says.

"I know," I say.

Next year, I will
be in the play.

⸙I LOVED THE PLAY⸙

so much that I go again
the next day.

It's the last show of the year.

This time I go alone. In my head,
I sing along, recite the lines I know,
and play the sheet music.

The music is in my bones.

ON MONDAY, YEARBOOKS

are passed around.

I flip to my photo.
There's more of me in the book.

Pictures of me at practice,
walking in the halls, and

eating in the cafeteria.
Considering how often

I missed school this last
year, I'm surprised but glad.

I mark the first blank page,
folding one corner over.

I'm saving the space
for my Dragons Club friends.

DURING LUNCH

the cafeteria buzzes with excitement.

Everyone is bouncing around from
table to table asking for signatures,
taking pictures, and hugging.

Within 45 minutes, nearly all
the pages in my yearbook are filled.

The first page has two messages:
One from Olivia in her loopy letters.

She wishes me the best of luck.
And the other is from Beth.

Her handwriting is small, sharp.
She says, "Glad we met!"

I write similar messages of our friendship,
how much they mean to me, and how this
year wouldn't have been the same.

Plus, hearts.

⌐FIRST CHAIR⌐

is the furthest thing from
my mind when I see the
student who has the title.

I don't know him well. His name
is Zhang Wei. I've heard him play,
and first chair is well-earned.

He stands out to me now because
of what Mr. Bernant said about
me losing first chair because
of issues at home.

I wonder about his life at home
and how we are more
than chair assignments.

I walk up to him and ask
him to sign my yearbook.

⤳ZHANG WEI⤺

signs my book.

He says, "I know you. You're good."

"Thank you," I say.
I feel my cheeks flush with heat.

"What happened to you?" he asks bluntly.

"Issues with my scholarship," I say.
I don't say any more than that.

"Oh, *you're* the other scholarship kid," he says.

He smiles at me.

THE OTHER
SCHOLARSHIP KID

That's me.

I remember how I used to feel
so weird about that label,
but now I just feel grateful.

Zhang and I smile
at each other awkwardly.

I wonder how he got into violin.

Does he have siblings?

For a moment there, I think he
wants to start up a conversation.

Like he's curious about my life, too.

Instead, he says, "Cool."
And he walks away.

I guess I'll see him next year.

THE SCHOOL YEAR IS OVER

I have a small break
before summer school begins.

I find out Olivia
is going to college
out of state.

She wants to spend
as much time as she can with Beth
and me before she goes.

SCHOOL COMES FIRST

I text Olivia back and tell her for sure.
I remind her school comes first though.

She says of course.

Mom picks up my supplies for summer school.
Violin practice is a given, but my

courses focus on general education
like math, English, history.

FINN SENDS ME AN EMAIL

He joined a local theater group
and asks if I'll watch their latest play.

I say yes and ask him how he's doing.
I'm glad to hear he's doing well.

He turned 18, got a job at a grocery
store, and now rents a room in a house.

He even enrolled at community college
for next year.

⚘EXERCISE IS IMPORTANT⚘

I jog and do yoga. I play my violin
more often, too.

Mr. Bernant's revelation about first chair
does inspire me. Not so much for

the title but to be the best I can be,
a personal promise to myself.

Emma is doing well. And Mom is home
more now, too. More present. More aware.

She watches us both more intensely now,
but I welcome the change.

THREE WEEKS INTO SUMMER SCHOOL

Emma is still drug free.
I count my blessings.

I feel more relaxed.
I can tell Mom is, too.

I'm thankful for the Dragons Club,
for what I learned about myself and

my family and all we have struggled with.
Things aren't perfect. They don't

have to be. Redirecting my anxiety
is an everyday thing.

But it has gotten easier.

⸙ TONIGHT, I MAKE DINNER ⸙

for Mom and Emma.
And for myself.

Spaghetti.

I boil the noodles and
make the sauce. I slice
up French bread, slather
it with butter, and add
garlic salt. I toss a
green salad, too.

I don't know what
tomorrow will bring.

But I have faith.

FOCUS ON MYSELF

I cannot prevent or control
anything outside of me.

But I can choose
how I handle things.

Loving someone doesn't mean
I should suffer because
of their actions.

Boundaries are okay.

Stay present.
Breathe.

Focus on myself.

MYSELF

Fingers on first and fourth, a whistle,
a song in the wind, on the waves.

I know what hope sounds like —
the support of my friends, my mom, and

healthy boundaries. I practice, and Emma listens
to this truth we faced together. And now I know that

no matter what happens, I have faith. I stand
on a rock, bow in one hand, violin in the other.

And serenity moves along the
scroll and tailpiece: I play my violin, for myself.

WANT TO KEEP READING?

If you liked this book, check out another book
from West 44 Books:

WATCHES AND WARNINGS
BY RYAN WOLF

ISBN: 9781538382714

THE
CELLAR

"It's always wise
to worry
about the wind.
When it gets
tired of our
little farms and schools
and grocery stores,
it will kick
them down.
It'll shake us
into the
sky."

Mr. Gregor likes
to talk this way
as we replace
old soup cans
with new ones
on his steel shelves.

We sweep
the concrete floors.
Check the dates
on medicines
in his first aid kits.
Drill together
new racks.
Fill them
with supplies.

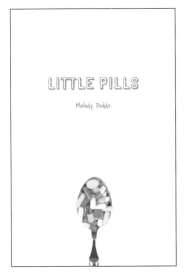

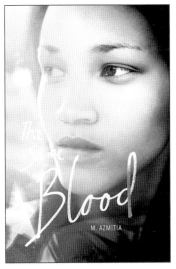

CHECK OUT MORE BOOKS AT:
www.west44books.com

An imprint of Enslow Publishing

WEST **44** BOOKS™

ABOUT THE AUTHOR

Cyn Bermudez is a writer from Bakersfield, California. She attended college in Santa Barbara, California, where she studied physics, film, and creative writing. She is the author of young adult verse novel *And the Moon Follows* and the hi-lo middle grade series Brothers. Cyn loves spending time with her family, baking, painting, crafting, and do-it-yourself projects. For more information about Cyn, visit her website at www.cynbermudez.com.